Table of Contents

Chapter 1

Heather rolled her high-backed office chair backward and folded her hands across her Donut Delights shirt. "I think it will be awesome," she said.

"I agree," Amy said, from the high stool beside her. She'd dragged that into the office from behind the counter, and perched there like an eagle to oversee the joint venture meeting. "People will love it. I'm pretty sure we could speak to the members of the town council, and they'd totally support it. Bring in loads more of those tourists I'm always complaining about."

"I've never heard you complain about tourists," Heather said and squinted up at her bestie.

"I can start," Ames replied.

Col Owen brushed his fingertips across his smooth tan forehead. "I like it. But what do we call it?"

The room fell silent, and all four occupants shared glances. They'd come this far in planning a festival, of sorts, but this detail had them stumped.

"Tea You Soon for Donuts," Col suggested.

Amy mock gagged. "Kill me now," she said, then winced. "Sorry." To say there'd been a rash of recent murders in their usually sleepy

Texan town was an understatement.

Hillside had boomed – tourists and investors had elbowed their way into Heather's beloved town and brought an economic boom, along with a scourge of unsavory types.

Though, she couldn't sum it up to just that, in all fairness.

Mona Petrov chewed her bottom lip and twisted a lock of her luxurious black hair around her finger. "Let's make it something simple. The 2017 Hillside Tea and Donut Fair," she said.

"I like that," Heather said and nodded toward Col's girlfriend. "I like it a lot."

"But if we put 2017 in there, that means we have to do it every year," Amy said. "That's quite a commitment." She drummed a beat on the legs of her jeans. "Oh yeah, I can't see myself performing in the 2030 Tea and Donut Fair."

"Performing?" Heather snorted. "Do I want to know what you mean by that?"

"I'd say there's a certain art to the glaze, Mrs. Shepherd," Amy replied.

Col laughed, and Mona frowned. They interchanged their reactions, then swapped back again. Their joint venture partners weren't accustomed to Heather and Amy's unique relationship just yet. They didn't know how to react to the jokes and insults.

"All right," Col said and scribbled on his Steno pad. "We're all agreed on the name?"

"Yes," Heather said.

Mona clapped to express her enthusiasm.

"Si," Amy said, just to be different.

"Great. That's settled. But when are we going to host this fair, and where? I suppose we could use the high school field."

"Oh, imagine we got a marching band," Amy said. "Like the High School marching band. We could have them –"

The door to Heather's office crashed open, and Kate Laverne marched into the room, bringing with her the scent of red velvet cupcakes and envy.

Angelica followed hot on her heels. "Sorry, I cannot stop her. She just go right past," she said. "I forget my rolling pin in the kitchen."

Col Owen's jaw dropped. "Rolling pin?"

"Don't worry," Amy said. "It's just a joke." She narrowed her eyes at the intruder, Miss Laverne. "For the most part."

"Heather Shepherd," Kate said and lifted her index finger. The finger of doom on her tipped with a bright red fingernail to match the crimson pants suit and black trench coat the woman wore.

"It's all right, Angelica," Heather said and smiled at her young assistant. "I'll handle this. Please make sure there are no further interruptions."

Angelica did a mini-curtsy-bow hybrid, then backed out of the room, staring rolling pins at the back of Kate Laverne's head. She clicked the office door shut.

"Kate," Heather said and didn't rise from her seat. She wasn't usually rude – she despised that more than any other negative form of behavior – but Laverne warranted it through and through.

One ill turn for another.

"I hear you're planning something without me," Laverne said, and strode forward another two steps on her crimson stilettos.

Amy hummed Devil in Disguise by Elvis Presley.

"Who is this woman?" Mona Petrov asked, and drew herself up straight as an ironing board.

Col placed a hand on her knee to calm her.

Kate Laverne's gaze met Mona's for the briefest moment. That was all it took for Laverne to dismiss her and focus on Heather once more. "You should know better than to try to hide this type of thing from me, Shepherd. The rumor mill in Hillside is fierce. It's true. It's –"

"Insert evil adjective here," Amy said.

"You shut your mouth," Kate growled and swung her finger of doom toward Heather's bestie.

"Enough," Heather said, quietly. "You've intruded on my personal space, a space where you will never be welcome. An insult is one step further and far enough. State your objective, then leave, Laverne, or I'll have you removed."

Mona sniffed her agreement.

Kate Laverne deflated like a tire with a leak. She licked her crimson lips, hesitated, and then narrowed her eyes. "I know you're going to do some big event. The whole town's talking about all the meetings you've been having with this hippie," she said, and jerked a thumb toward Col. "What's happening."

"Hippie!" Col sat upright.

Heather raised her palm and pushed it outward to maintain the peace. She didn't remove her gaze from Laverne's face, however. What a truly infuriating human being she'd turned out to be.

Back in New York, Laverne had been a thorn in her side at best. In Hillside, she'd upgraded to a cactus. Several cacti filled with bitter fluid.

"Kate, our business venture has nothing to do with you."

"It's a festival of some kind, isn't it?" Kate asked. Perceptive she was, tactful she was not.

"It's none of your business," Col said.

Kate ignored him too. Perhaps, she'd dismissed him as an unworthy adversary. "I want in on it," she said.

"Pardon?" Heather blinked.

Amy's jaw dropped.

"I want in. You're not hosting a food festival without my cupcakes," she said.

"No," Col said, and Mona chimed in with him.

"That's two votes against you," Heather said. "I hold the third."

"And I hold a quarter," Amy said. "I vote no."

Heather channeled her inner Simon Cowell. "It's going to be a no from me," she said, in her best impersonation.

"Oh good one," Amy whispered.

Kate Laverne huffed and puffed. Her cheeks reddened, her eyes bulged, and her heels tapped a beat on the wooden boards. "You'll regret this," she said. "I swear it on – on – my business."

And with that, Miss Laverne turned on her painfully tall stiletto heel and charged from Heather's office.

Chapter 2

Heather sat on her stool behind the cash register and wriggled her nose from side-to-side. Something about today felt off. Donut sales were up, sure, and the Pecan Nut Crunch Donuts, her new creation, were a hit.

She'd taught all the assistants how to make it early that morning.

A delicious baked vanilla base, interspersed with hard bits of caramel, dipped in a caramel glaze and coated in pecan nuts. They'd sold themselves, and Heather and Maricela had spent the morning handing out Col

Owen's freebie vouchers for tea at his shop.

"What's the matter?" Amy asked, and plopped down in the stool next to Heather's – the same she'd had in the office that morning.

Ames had taken to sitting in on meetings. Heather trusted her opinion, as sarcastic as it could be, and Amy's presence kept Heather clear and level headed. After all, only one of them could act like a good at any given time.

The more Amy goofed, the less Heather could.

"Hello? Heather?" Amy wiggled her hand in front of Heather's nose. "Is this about ol' crazy Kate? I hope you're not letting that woman get to you."

Heather laughed and shook her head. "No. Kate doesn't bother me. Her cupcake store doesn't bother me, and her foul attitude... I'd be lying if I said that didn't bother me, but that's just because she's a rude person. And you know how I feel about rude people," she said.

"Then what's bothering you?" Amy asked.

Heather pointed to Eva Schneider's empty table. "Eva hasn't come in to taste my new treat today," she said and checked her filigree watch – a gift from her husband. "And it's almost noon."

Amy's brow wrinkled. "Okay, that is kind of weird."

Eva came in each morning with her Hillside Reporter. She'd never missed a day since Heather had opened Donut Delights, apart from the horrible few weeks she'd spent in a coma in Hillside Regional.

Heather shuddered at the memory. She squished her phone out of her pocket. "I'm calling her house. I don't like this, Ames. Eva wouldn't stay away. She loves finding out the new donut flavor each week."

"Hey, but isn't it library day today? She always gets her books on a Monday," Amy said, and a tinge of hope entered her tone.

"She wouldn't hang around in the library for this long," Heather replied. She scrolled through her contacts and tapped Eva's name. She put the phone to her ear.

One ring, two, three, and four. A click and a beep.

"Hello, you've reached Mrs. Schneider. Please leave a message after the tone." Eva's sweet voice traveled down the line.

It didn't have its usual soothing effect on Heather.

"She didn't answer?" Amy asked. She hopped off her stool and paced to the coffee machine. She pushed buttons and gathered cups, for incoming customers.

"No answer." Heather's insides twisted into a knot. She shouldn't panic like this. Eva was a grown woman, for heaven's sake.

The phone buzzed in Heather's palm and she lifted it. Ryan's name flashed on the screen. The blood drained from her face.

"Oh no," she whispered. "No, no. I won't think that. It can't be."

"What's the matter?" Amy asked. "Who's calling?"

Heather didn't dare show Ames' the caller ID. She'd likely have a full blown meltdown. She swiped her trembling thumb across the green icon, instead. "Hello?"

"Hey," Ryan said. "I've got some bad news."

The interior of the store spun around in front of her and she squeezed her eyes shut to block it out. The panic didn't subside. "What's going on?"

"There's been a murder."

"Who?"

"One of the librarians at the Hillside Library was crushed by a bookshelf. You know, one of those massive things. Weighed a ton," Ryan said.

"A librarian?" Heather's eyes snapped open and sound rushed back into her ears. She sucked in a deep breath. "Just a librarian."

"Yeah," he said. "And your friend Eva was there to witness it."

"Oh my gosh, is she okay?" Heather asked.

Amy fumbled the cups on the coffee machine's silver grate.

"She's fine. A little shaken up, but fine," Ryan replied. "I was hoping you could send someone over with a few donuts for her, actually."

"I can come –"

"Not you, hon. I need your help with the case," Ryan said and huffed a sigh. "This one's tricky. Can you meet me at the library in a half hour? Bring a mug of coffee?"

"Sure," Heather said, no problem. She could breathe again, at least, now that she knew Eva was safe. "I'll see you then," she said and hung up.

"Is she all right?" Amy asked.

Maricela stepped forward to greet a customer and give them both a break. Her assistant to the rescue, as usual.

"She's at the station. Apparently, she witnessed a murder," Heather said, and the beginnings of intrigue tugged at the end of the chromosome which held her sleuthin' gene.

"A murder!" Amy said, a little too loudly.

The woman who'd ordered a donut gasped.

"Just talking about a movie," Amy said. "Uh, something by Stephen King."

The customer accepted her donut and scooted off to her table, glancing backward every few steps.

"Huh, I don't think she bought it."

"Of course she didn't buy it," Heather said. "Everyone knows we investigate murders here."

"What happened?" Amy asked.

"I'm not entirely sure, just yet," Heather said. "But a librarian was killed. Ryan mentioned a bookshelf. I've got to get over there now and help him out, but he asked if someone could take over some donuts for Eva while she's there."

"I'll do it," Amy said, immediately. "Totally. Oh gosh, this probably shocked her. She needs some sugar in her system."

"I don't know about that," Heather said. "Eva's a strong woman. She's survived a lot and thrived because of it. I sometimes get the feeling that she'll outlive me."

Amy laughed and scooted off toward the kitchen to rustle up some special Pecan Nut Crunch Donuts for their favorite customer.

Heather tapped Maricela on the shoulder. "I'll be back later to lock up, okay?"

"Sure, boss. No problem. I hold down the fort," she said.

Maricela and Angelica's English had improved in leaps and bounds over the past year. Heather smiled at her assistant then swept around the counter and toward the front door, curiosity driving her steps.

Another week, another case. What would this one bring?

Chapter 3

Heather folded her arms and tapped her heeled boot on the green carpet. "What was her name?" She asked.

The building was eerily quiet, without the rustle of pages or the hushed whispers and steps of Hillside folks out to pick up a copy of the latest and greatest, or one of the classics.

A green banker's lamp illuminated the checkout counter and cast light on the fallen bookshelves.

Ryan flipped up a sheet on his notepad. "Helena Chadwick," he said. "New librarian. She'd only worked here for a week before it happened."

"And how, may I ask, did it – uh, you know –"

Ryan directed the end of his pen toward the two fallen bookshelves. "As far as we can tell, the right one toppled onto her, and the left followed. She was caught in between."

"That must've made a lot of noise. And taken a lot of effort to pull off," Heather said. "If they're heavy enough to kill a woman, then surely they must be darn heavy to push over."

"I agree," Ryan said. "We haven't had them weighed yet, but the verdict is this must've been done by a man."

"Or a woman who had leverage," Heather replied. She mimed inserting a crowbar beneath the shelf and tipping it forward.

"Good point," Ryan said and scribbled down a note on his pad.

Heather turned in a slow circle, her hands tucked behind her back. She looked up at the second floor, empty of chairs, but overlooking the first with rails and platforms open to the air. "No witnesses?"

"Only Eva and one other, but he was further back in the library,"

Ryan said. "In one of those book alcove things."

Heather had sat in an alcove a few weeks back, ironically enough, and she'd heard nothing but the woman in front of her at the time, and seen only books, shelves and the written word.

"Yeah, he definitely didn't see anything if he was where he said he was," Heather said. "Only two people?"

"Nobody reads here anymore," Ryan said. "They've all got those tablet doo-hickeys."

"I'm going to put aside the fact that you just used the word doo-hickey, to point out that the tablet you're talking about is a Kindle. A Kindle, my good man," Heather said and faced her husband. She winked at him. "You barbarian."

He chuckled and inserted the pen between his lips. He sucked on the end then removed it and swirled it around in the air. "Would've been useful if there'd been someone up top to witness this."

"Wait, you said only two people," Heather replied.

"Oh yeah, and the other librarian," he said. "Lady in glasses. Her name is, gosh, what's her name?" He flipped through his notes again. "Sorry, it's been a long day. This happened at 9 am, if you can believe it."

"That's not exactly a prime murder time," Heather agreed. She'd investigated enough murders to qualify that they usually occurred in the evening, though, in truth, murder didn't fit any molds.

Other than the dark, seeping kind. Blegh.

"The other librarian was Martha Rizzo. She said she was placing returned books on the shelves at the time of the murder. She heard the crash, but she didn't see what happened. She was the one who called the cops," Ryan said.

Heather licked her lips. She hadn't brought out her tablet to take notes just yet. Ryan would forward her a dossier with all the relevant information later in the day or the very next morning anyway.

For now, she could work hands-free.

"Do we know anything about our victim? Any information which might help us pin down an enemy, a potential murderer?"

"That's the thing," Ryan said. "We know nothing. She was from out of town, and her co-librarian said she wasn't exactly the talkative type."

"Huh. Out of town. Which city?"

"No clue," Ryan said. "But we did find something interesting on her arm."

"What was that?"

"A diamond tennis bracelet," he replied. "And there was a shaded outline of what looked like a ring on her left finger."

"An engagement ring that'd been removed?" Heather asked.

Ryan shrugged. "Your guess is as good as mine. But I'll put this to you, a woman who works in a library shouldn't be able to afford a diamond tennis bracelet."

"Unless she's got a rich family," Heather said. "Or has her own business one the side."

"Sure, but then she wouldn't be anonymous," Ryan replied. "We wouldn't struggle to pin down her identity."

Heather conceded the point with a smile. She loved sleuthin' with her husband. They had an easy repartee which helped Heather brainstorm ideas and solutions to their challenges.

"Fingerprints?" Heather asked.

"Yeah, they've already dusted," Ryan said. "We'll have the results back when we have them back if you know what I mean."

Heather dropped into a crouch beside the fallen bookcases and examined the underside of the shelf closest to her. A series of scratches scarred the wooden underside. Parallel white lines scraped on the brown. "Take a look at this," she said.

"What is it?" Ryan's standard issue shoes thumped on the carpet and came to a halt beside her. He crouched too, and bathed her in the scent of clean, starched shirts and used paper.

"Markings," Heather said. "I'd be willing to be anything that the killer used some form of leverage."

"So we're looking for a crowbar," Ryan said.

Heather ran her fingers through the grooves. "Anything which could've made these marks." That didn't exactly narrow down their suspect list, but it was the best she could do, given the circumstances.

"I'll make a note of it," Ryan said.

Heather sighed and rose from her crouch. This would be interesting, to say the least, and she doubted a self-defense case would stand here. Pushing over a shelf didn't scream, "Help me, I'm under attack."

At least she knew where to start, this time.

Chapter 4

Eva flapped her hands at the crowd of assistants around her table. "Please, dears, I'm fine, I'm fine."

"We worry about you, Eva," Maricela said, her hands tucked into the front pocket of her Donut Delights apron. Jung mirrored her sentiment with a doleful bob of his head.

"I assure you, I'm quite all right," Eva said, and patted her blue-colored hair do. "Heavens, I haven't had this much attention all at once in ages." Two bright pinks spots appeared on the apples of her cheeks.

"All right everyone," Heather said, from her seat at the table across from Eva. "It's time to get back to work and give Eva some breathing room."

A day had passed since Eva's questioning at the police station over the strange murder in the Hillside Public Library, but she'd recovered from the shock pretty well.

The assistants hurried off to their stations – Ken and Maricela behind the counter, and Emily, Jung, and Angelica back into the kitchen. Amy kept her seat, for now – she'd just started her break.

"You want to know what happened," Eva said, immediately. "I'm happy to talk about it dear. It didn't scare me at all."

Heather exhaled – she'd worried Eva would've been scarred by the trauma of the murder, but then, as she'd said yesterday, Eva was a strong woman. She'd been through worse and lost more than a few hours in a police station.

Heather dragged her tablet out of her bag and placed it on the tabletop. "Gosh, I'd never thought I'd interview you like this, Eva."

"Me neither, dear. But I'm happy to help."

Amy chewed on a donut and swallowed, loudly. "We're just glad you're okay. We freaked out yesterday when you didn't come in at your usual time."

"I wish I could've called to let you know what'd happened," Eva said. "But at least I get my donut now." She picked a pecan off the top of the caramel glaze and popped it into her mouth.

Heather grinned at her oldest customer and tapped on her Evernote App. She couldn't get over how much the tablet had helped her during her investigations. She'd messed up a few leads here and there, missed a connection or two, but boy, at least she didn't waste paper and blot her fingers full of ink anymore.

"Let's start from the beginning," Heather said. "You went to the library yesterday."

"Yes dear, I went at about 8 am and collected a few of my favorite books. I checked them out with the lovely lady at the front," Eva said.

"Which one?" Heather asked. "What was her name?"

"Oh, I can't recall what her name was, but it wasn't the poor woman who died," Eva said. "The other librarian, Helena, was packing books away. I went to sit down at a table quite close to her, but my back was to the shelves."

"And then what happened?" Heather asked, and typed notes on her screen.

Eva rolled her top lip over her bottom. "I read for a while. I like to settle down with my books and work up a bit of an appetite for when I come through to Donut Delights."

Heather waited for Eva to continue. She used the pause to take a sip of her coffee.

"Then I heard the woman, that Helena, say something like, oh what was it?" Eva scratched her temple. "No, I'm not leaving. I've told you a hundred times."

Heather typed that onto her notepad too. Amy arched her eyebrow and scooched forward on her seat. "Sounds like she knew the murderer."

"Or she knew someone in the building," Heather said. "How long after that did the shelf fall over?"

"About five minutes, I would say, though I wasn't exactly keeping track of the time," Eva replied. "I heard a shuffle and a creak. I didn't think anything of it. But then there was this horrendous scratching noise, and then it happened. A bang." Eva shuddered – a delicate shake of her shoulder.

Amy offered her a bite of her donut.

Eva smiled but didn't take her up on the offer.

"Did you see anything else, Eva?" Heather asked, her fingers hovering above the tablet's screen and the mix of words – some misspelled – scrawled across it.

"Not really," she said.

"Who was at the library?" Amy asked, and licked the glaze off her fingers. "What types of people did you see?"

"It's usually empty on a Monday morning, that early," Eva said, and screwed up her eyes, trying to grab at a memory. "Oh wait, I did see one strange guy hanging around. Oh yes!"

"A strange guy?" Heather asked.

"Yes, I remember him specifically because he stood out. He hovered around outside the library as I entered."

"What made him strange?"

"He had a black Mohawk," Eva said. "I'm not one of those super conservative types, but I do believe a man should cover his head all the way around, or else, shave it off completely. This hair looked to be a fashion statement."

Heather typed it all out.

"Oh, and he had a diamond ring in his nose."

"A diamond ring," Heather mused. Diamonds had come up a lot in the last two days. Diamond tennis bracelets. An engagement ring. And now this, what did it all mean?

"Heather," Amy said and downed the last of her coffee. "We've got another meeting in a few minutes."

"Right!" She'd totally forgotten about their appointment with Col Owen in his tea shop. Hopefully,

Kate Laverne wouldn't burst in on them on foreign ground. The last time had been memorable, to say the least.

Shoot, if only she'd planned better – now, she didn't have enough time to finish off the interview with Eva.

"Don't worry, dear, I'll be here if you need anything else," the old woman said and patted her on the arm. "You go ahead and plan your fair. I can't wait until the day it starts."

Chapter 5

The inside of Col Owen's Tea Shop had that same cool, green vibe which soothed Heather. She'd been on edge ever since she'd interviewed Eva in Donut Delights. The case sat in the back of her brain, brewing like the tea in the china pot in the center of their table.

"- this Sunday," Col said.

"What now?" Heather sat up straight and stared at him. "Are you talking about the date?"

"That's right," Col replied, he glanced at the empty chair beside him. Mona had gone out to run a few errands. It was strange seeing him without her. They'd been glued to each other's sides for the weeks that Heather had known them.

"This Sunday is too soon," Amy said. "Way too soon. We haven't even contacted the committee yet. We haven't spoken to the high school for the band. Or advertised it. We can't do this Sunday."

"I want this up and running as fast as we can achieve it." Col set his jaw.

"What's the problem?" Heather asked. "Why's there such a rush to get it done?"

Col massaged his left shoulder with one hand and rolled his head from side to side. "I've got a few things on my mind. A deadline. I guess you could call it that."

"What kind of deadline?" Amy asked.

Col's scratched the back of his neck this time and looked out of the green glass window. He cleared his throat, twice. "I'm going to ask Mona to marry me," he said. "Soon. I want to do it real soon."

Amy clapped her hands together. "That's fantastic. I'm so happy for you."

"Me too," Heather said and squeezed Col's forearm. "I understand why you want to get the fair out of the way, but I don't think this weekend is plausible."

Amy bit her bottom lip. "The man's got to propose, Heather."

"I know," Heather replied. "We can try to hustle it along and do it next Sunday."

"I could work with that," Col said. "Maybe I'll even propose then." He lifted the teapot to pour a little more tea into his cup. He weighed it and shrugged. "I'll brew us another pot."

Col creaked out of his rickety chair and shuffled to the counters at the far end of the 'service area' of his store, teapot in hand.

Amy watched him go, then leaned toward her friend. "Are you okay? You seem distracted."

"Got the case on my mind," Heather replied and tapped her temple. "As always." She'd had issues with her one track mind for a while. She could only focus her attention fully on one thing at once, and sometimes the other areas of her life and business suffered as a result.

But she'd work on it. She'd try, at least.

"The case. Have you found out anything else? Gotten your dossier from Ryan yet?"

"No," Heather said. "But I'm sure he'll give it to me today sometime. I just think the whole set up is strange. Why did the murderer kill Helena in the library? Why not somewhere more discrete? It's like they were looking for attention."

"Why?" Amy asked.

"That's what I've got to figure out. And get this, the victim had a diamond tennis bracelet on," Heather said.

"Oh gosh, that's my fantasy item. One day when I'm rich and

famous I'll have one," Amy said and clasped her hands in front of her chest. She batted her eyelids. "That's weird, though." She dropped the act. "She was a librarian. Why did she have a diamond tennis bracelet?"

"That's not all. There was evidence that she'd worn an engagement ring but had taken it off. A tan line, apparently."

"Diamonds are a girl's best friend, right?"

"What are you two talking about?" Col asked, and strode back, teapot in hand. He placed it in the center of the table.

An awkward silence fell. Heather discussed cases with Ames because she was her assistant. Her partner in crime, excuse the pun. She couldn't share with her joint venture partner.

"I see," Col said. "Well, I heard diamonds and tennis bracelets. Does it have anything to do with the robbery at Krakowski's?"

"A robbery?" Amy asked.

"Yeah, you know that jewelry store down the road. They're just off the main street. Jones Krakowski is the owner. He's always lobbying the town board for something or the other. A real shouter."

"Shouter?"

"Yeah, wants it done his way or the highway." Col shrugged and put down the teapot in the center of the table, next to the arrangement of flowers at its center. "Apparently, someone broke into his store and made off with a whole bunch of stuff. Cops didn't catch them, and Krakowski had a fit because they thought he did it to get the insurance money."

"And he doesn't need the insurance money?" Heather asked.

"No way, no how. The guy is loaded. He's got a mansion on the outskirts of town. His wife stays there all day long," Col said.

"Interesting," Heather said and tapped her chin with the side of her index finger. "Very interesting. I think I should pay this Mr. Krakowski a visit." At worst, she'd find out more about who might've stolen the diamonds from his store.

Ryan hadn't mentioned the robbery to her, and she hadn't picked up a newspaper in ages, simply because of the joint venture and the cases. Between that and looking after Lils and the animals, there wasn't much time for keeping abreast of current events.

She'd have to change that.

"Now, about next Sunday," Col said.

But Heather's mind had already drifted back to the case. Luckily, she had Amy to step in and organize for her.

Chapter 6

Krakowski's name stood out in sparkling silver print on the brick overhang above the caged entrance. Behind the box windows, a collection of watches and rings, bracelets and golden, tear drop necklaces sparkled on red velvet cushions.

A Tag Heuer advert, Leonardo DiCaprio as the subject, stood behind the display.

"Don't hate me because you ain't me," Amy said.

"Pardon?"

"That's what Leo's advert says. Get a watch and be cool like him," Amy said. "As if anyone could be cool like Leo DiCaprio."

"I hear he's doing a lot of good things for the environment," Heather replied and strode toward the front gate of the jewelry store.

"Yeah? Tell that to the bear in the Revenant." Amy followed her to the cage door.

Heather pressed a pearlescent knob beside the door, and a buzzer sounded inside. Two minutes passed, and a man shuffled out of the back room, dressed in a tuxedo and a top hat.

A top hat.

"Wow," Amy said. "I don't know what to say. I've lost my will to be sarcastic."

The man swept his hat off his head and strode through the center of his store. He halted in front of the second gate and glared at them. "And who, may I ask, are you?"

"Mr. Krakowski?" Heather kept her hands at her sides. This guy had to be jumpy after the recent break-in at his store.

"Who's asking?" The man said and narrowed his ice blue eyes to slits. He was handsome in his own way, silver-haired with a neatly trimmed beard. "You a thief?"

"No, Mr. Krakowski. I'm Heather Shepherd. I'm a private investigator working as a consultant for the Hillside Police Department." She'd practiced the words over and over again. They slipped from her tongue as easy as 'donuts.'

"Investigating what?" Krakowski asked, in gravelly tones. "You didn't do anything when I was robbed. So, what have you got to investigate now?"

"The murder of Helena Chadwick," Heather replied, evenly.

Krakowski stiffened. "Helena," he breathed and gripped the bars of the second cage door in his fists.

His knuckles turned white from the pressure. "Helena Chadwick."

"I think he knows her," Amy said.

"Oh, I knew her, all right. That little miss was the woman who stole from my store. She's the one who needed to be arrested," Krakowski said. "Guess it's too late for that now."

Heather readjusted her tote's straps on her shoulder. Clearly, Mr. Krakowski didn't plan on letting them into his store. "You think she stole from you?" She asked.

"I know she stole from me. That woman was a thief. She came into to town in the middle of the night. I'm sure of it. And she got that job in the library to make it seem like she was an innocent. But I knew the truth."

"What made you think she did it?" Heather asked.

"She used to hang around in the street outside and stare at my rings."

"The engagement rings?" Amy stepped to one side and peered at that particular selection. Diamonds glimmered against platinum and gold bands.

"That's right," Krakowski said.

"And some of the rings were stolen?" Heather asked.

"No." Krakowski turned his top hat upside down and bopped the inside of it with a fist. "No, but other things were stolen. One of my tiaras, bracelets, necklaces. A priceless timepiece from the civil war era."

"A tennis bracelet?" Heather asked.

Krakowski grunted agreement. "Yes, a tennis bracelet and many others like it. The woman was a thief. A dirty thief and I –"

Heather waved a hand to cut him off. She'd heard the rhetoric before – he'd say he was glad she was gone, but he'd never have dreamed of hurting her.

"Mr. Krakowski, where were you on Monday morning?" Heather asked.

"I was at home. I had one of my assistants come in to open the store," he replied, in clipped tones.

"Can anyone confirm your whereabouts?" Heather asked.

"Of course," he said, and tugged on either lapel of his suit. "My wife was with me. Speak to her if you need confirmation."

That wasn't a strong alibi, but it would have to do for now.

"Do you know of anyone who would've wanted to hurt Helena Chadwick?" Heather asked.

"I don't know much about the woman. Only that she was a thief and you and the police did nothing to stop her. She was probably a criminal." Krakowski placed his top hat back on top of his neat haircut. "Now, if you'll excuse me. I have a shop to get back to."

Krakowski spun on his heel and marched back toward the counter at the back of his store.

Heather chewed her lip and backed away from the first gate.

"What do you think?" Amy asked, and flicked her short blond hair back.

"I don't like it. I don't like the sound of this one bit," Heather whispered. "Krakowski believed Helena stole from him and begrudged the cops their inability to act on what happened."

"Meaning?"

"Meaning, he has a motive. He could've taken matters into his own hands," Heather said. "Eva told us that Helena spoke with someone just moments before the bookshelves fell over. It could've been him."

Amy linked her arm through Heather's, and they strolled down the sidewalk together. "Let's go check out the alibi," Amy said and patted Heather's forearm. "If he says he was home, we should find out if it's true."

"Assuming his wife will tell us the truth," Heather replied. She fished her cell out of her pocket and shot off a text to her husband.

"What are you doing?" Amy asked.

"Asking my contact for Krakowski's home address," Heather replied. "Unless you've got a phone book in your pocket."

"I'm all out," Amy said and patted herself down. "I've got gum, though."

Heather chuckled and led the way back to her Chevrolet Spark.

Chapter 7

The Chevrolet's tires crunched on the gravel which led up to the massive front porch of the mansion, hidden among the trees.

Amy rolled down her window and stuck her head out. "It's cold," she said, "But it sure is beautiful."

A fountain sat directly in front of the stone steps which led onto the porch. Water tinkled from the head of a lovely maiden and dribbled down her slender form into the basin below.

Evergreens surrounded the house, shading it from the sun and protecting it from unwanted eyes. Not that anyone on the Highway on the way into Hillside would glare up at the house.

Heather stopped the car and pulled up the parking brake. "It's unbelievable," she said and leaned on her steering wheel to take in the entirety of the three-story home.

"I can't believe Krakowski freaked out about a few diamonds. He's obviously making a killing," Amy said.

"I don't see how. This is Hillside, not one of the big-time cities where the celebrities shop," Heather said. She tapped her thumbs on the sides of her steering wheel, inhaling the scent of her lavender car air freshener. "Only one way to find out, I guess."

Heather opened her door and got out and scattered a few stones with her boots. Cool air whipped her hair back, but it wasn't icy. The trees blocked the breeze for the most part.

Amy followed her out and gazed at the bruised clouds overhead. "Storm's coming," she said.

The pre-rain moisture clung to the air and brought back Heather's memories of baking with her grandmother. They'd spent many a storm huddled in front of a gas stove, creating glazes and fudges, and even a ganache.

During one violent storm, the power had cut out, and they'd been forced to mix a glaze by candlelight, cackling like two witches in front of a cauldron.

A tiny smile lifted the corners of Heather's lips.

"I love the smell of rain," she said.

"I love the smell of rain and donuts. I think they go well together, don't you?" Amy asked. "We'll have to get some after this."

They crunched across the gravel and up the front stairs. Amy stopped to dig a bit of gravel out of the ridges on the sole of her shoe.

Heather pressed the button beside the intercom.

"Hello?" A woman's voice crackled through the silver speaker. "Hello, who is it?"

"Hi, this is Heather Shepherd. I'm working with the Hillside Police Department. I need to speak with Mrs. Krakowski."

"All right," the woman said. "Come in. It's unlocked."

Heather blinked at Ames.

Her bestie straightened with the piece of gravel wedged between her thumb and forefinger. "Got it," she said.

Heather pressed the intercom button again. "I — uh, we should just enter?"

"Yeah. I'm in the living room. It's the fifth door on your right. If you hit the stairs, you've gone too far," said the woman, who had to be Mrs. Krakowski.

Heather hurried forward and depressed the curved golden door handle on the right-hand side. The door opened on a grand lobby, which suited a hotel more than a home. It yawned upward, encompassing all three stories and framed by the railings of the halls which overlooked it.

Heather whistled.

"Wow," Amy said. "Are you sure we're at the right address?"

"Count the doors," Heather replied.

They entered, and the front door swung shut behind them with a clang. Amy jumped and grabbed hold of Heather's arm. She giggled and let it go again, then brushed off the front of her puffy blue jacket.

"Fifth door on the left," Heather said and paced across the polished wooden floor toward the grand staircase ahead.

She peered into each doorway and caught a glimpse of a living room, a bathroom, a study, a bedroom and then... Mrs. Krakowski herself, draped across a sofa, a plaid blanket covering her legs.

"Hello," she said, with a bright smile. "Please, come in." She readjusted the sparkling tiara on top of her dyed platinum blond hair. Wrinkles around her eyes and mouth placed her at around fifty.

She had to be about ten years younger than her husband.

Heather didn't meet Amy's gaze. She'd only prompt a shocked stare or an inappropriate joke if she did.

"Please," Mrs. Krakowski repeated.

Heather walked into the living room and halted beside an armchair. "Mrs. Krakowski?"

"That's right," she said. "Sorry I didn't come to the door. I've been feeling ill of late. I don't get around much." A pile of books teetered on the coffee table beside her sofa.

"I'm sorry to hear that," Heather said and took a seat. Amy followed her lead but didn't say a word. She hadn't taken her eyes off the tiara since they'd entered. "I hope you don't mind the intrusion."

"Not at all," Mrs. Krakowski said. "How many I help you."

"I'm hearing investigating the murder of Helena Chadwick," Heather said. "Did you know her?"

Mrs. Krakowski looked out of the window at the far end of the room, at the trees, their branches brushed by the winds which came before a Hillside storm. "No," she said, at last. "No idea."

"Your husband seemed to think Helena stole from him," Heather replied.

Mrs. Krakowski sighed. "Jones thinks many things," she said.

"Some of them aren't wise to talk about."

What on earth did that mean?

Heather coughed into her fist, but Mrs. Krakowski didn't shift from her position.

"There's a storm coming," she said, after a moment. Her lightning blue eyes, similar to her husband's, fixed on Heather, at last. "What did you want to ask me?"

"Where was your husband two days ago? On the morning of Helena Chadwick's death."

Mrs. Krakowski adjusted the tiara in her hair. A flicker of sorrow dragged at her porcelain fine features. "He was here, of course. Where else would he have been?"

"You'd be willing to testify in court on that?" Heather asked, and hardened her tone.

The woman sat up straighter. "Has it come to that?"

"Not yet," Heather said. "But if I can't figure out who might have harmed Helena, it might." She pushed hard because she didn't have any other lead but Krakowski and his disdain for the librarian.

Hopefully, Ryan would have more information for her this evening, after work.

"I don't know what to tell you," the woman said. "He was here. He's always here at that time of the morning."

"Why?" Amy asked.

"Because he has to give me my medication and lecture me about drinking fluids. Then he's gone for the day," Mrs. Krakowski replied. "Gone and I don't see him unless I stay up very late. My husband is dedicated to his store."

Dedicated enough to linger for hours? How on earth had the jewelry thief pulled off the heist then?

"I think that will be all for now, Mrs. Krakowski," Heather said. "Thank you for your time."

They'd lingered long enough already, and Heather had to get back to the store and make sure everything had run smoothly that morning.

"Of course," Mrs. Krakowski said. "I've got plenty of reading to keep me busy. Oh, and if you need evidence that my husband was here when he said he was, just check the surveillance cameras."

Heather could've kicked herself. A mansion like this was bound to have surveillance.

Chapter 8

Heather tucked her feet underneath herself in her classic position on the sofa in her living room. It'd been a long day — running back and forth from the store to Krakowski's Jewelers and then out to see his wife. She clutched a cup of Chai tea to her chest and inhaled the soothing aromas.

Cinnamon, cardamom, clove and just a hint of black pepper. Col Owen's love of tea had rubbed off on her, and she'd bought a bag of the stuff from him for home use.

"We can do it at the end of the week," Ryan said, to Lilly.

Their daughter hovered in the doorway, outfitted in her pink PJs and fluffy slippers, Cupcake tucked against her chest.

"What's going on?" Heather asked. She'd totally zoned out for a second there. The dinner, a delicious pasta carbonara prepared by Ryan, settled in her stomach and rocked her to sleep.

"It's Nicolas' birthday on Sunday," Lilly said. "And I really want to throw him a party at the shelter. He's the kid who lost both his parents in a car accident."

Heather bit back a gasp. "Yeah, we can do that Lils. We can throw a donut party if you like."

Ryan chuckled. "Does that settle it? Are you happy to ascend to your chambers, madam?"

"Sheesh, Dad, talk like a human," Lilly said and stuck out her tongue. "Thanks a lot. I think Nicolas will be really happy. He hasn't had a lot to be happy about lately."

"Don't forget it's your birthday in a few weeks," Heather said. "You've got to figure out what you want to do," Heather replied.

"I will," Lilly said. "Maybe like a trip somewhere?" Lilly blew Heather a kiss, then hurried out of the room and up the stairs. Dave hopped off the sofa and tailed her, his claws ticking on the hardwood floors.

Heather took another sip of her tea and swirled the flavorful liquid around her mouth before swallowing. "At least she's happy."

Ryan strolled to the sofa and sat down beside her. He slipped his arm around her shoulders. "And you're not?"

"I am. I'm confused about the case, but yes, I'm happy." She lived in an awesome house with people and animals she adored. How could she not be happy?

"Confused is the right word for it. We haven't found anything that matches those markings on the underside of the bookcase," Ryan said.

"Have you gotten back the results of the analysis?" Heather asked, and her wedding band clicked against the side of the mug.

"Yeah, and they're not clearing anything up. No fingerprints that we can identify and even if we could, I don't think it would be much of a lead. We can't pinpoint who might've come and gone in the library the day before."

"No surveillance?" Heather asked.

"Whatever system they have is so old it went on the fritz months before this happened. No news on when it will be repaired," Ryan said.

"So, no prints, no footage, and no matches for the scratches on the underside of the bookcase," Heather said. "We're stumped."

"I wouldn't say that. We've still got people to interview. I picked up on a rumor that the local jeweler was robbed a few days before the murder," Ryan said.

"Wait a second; you picked up on the rumor?" Heather asked. "Mr. Krakowski said he reported the theft to the police."

"Nope," Ryan replied and shrugged his shoulders. "Looks

like Mr. Krakowski lied. You already spoke to him, then."

"Yeah. Col told me that same rumor this afternoon, and I followed up on it," Heather said. "I spoke to Krakowski's wife too, and she gave us the surveillance tapes which prove the jeweler was at home at the time of the murder. Or the butler gave them to us on her orders."

"The butler," Ryan said, in a monotone.

"That's right. She has a butler. Amy almost passed out. She couldn't handle the glitz and glam." The tapes had shown them exactly what both Krakowski's had claimed – Jones had been home at the time of the murder.

He couldn't possibly have pushed over the bookshelf. Which left no one that knew, and Eva without a lead for her, apart from –

"Oh! Did Eva tell you about the stranger she saw?" Heather asked.

"The guy with the Mohawk, yeah," Ryan replied. "We don't know who he is, yet, but we've got people out watching for him, particularly around the library."

"Great," Heather said. Though, she didn't feel great. Nothing about the situation felt great.

"That only leaves me with one option."

"And what's that?"

"Speak to the other librarian, of course," Heather replied. She'd yet to press the woman for information. Hopefully, Miss Rizzo would offer up something useful. A case breaker, even.

After all, she'd been in the library at the time of her colleague's death.

Chapter 9

The Hillside Public Library was open to the good folks of Hillside once again. People didn't exactly stream in and out the doors, but a crowd of teens pushed past Amy on their way up the stairs.

"Hey," Amy said. "Old people walking over here."

The kids ignored her.

"We're not old people," Heather said. "We're young at heart."

"That just means we're old on the outside," Amy replied and pinched the skin on her cheek. She pulled it away from her face and let it settle back. "Look at that. It takes for every to bounce back. You know you're on the way out when your skin does that."

"Don't be so negative."

"Is it negative? Is it? Or am I being a realist?" Amy countered.

"I think all this fresh air is getting to you," Heather replied. The storm still hadn't come, and she'd have done anything for the pressure to break and those first drops of rain to patter from the heavens and wet the top of her head.

They'd had a rash of winter storms, lately, but Hillside had a history of those.

Heather imagined it was the last struggle for control between an angry, deluded Winter and the new shoots of Spring.

They entered the open doors of the library and hurried toward the front counter, where a middle-aged woman sat, her wire-frame glasses pinched on the tip of her hooked nose.

Martha Rizzo wore her bright red hair in a tight, ballerina bun on top of her head. A few bobby pins held the stray strands in place. Meticulous, really, apart from the jelly stain down the front of her steel gray sweater.

The teens who'd practically shoved them down the stairs –

okay, bumped – giggled and gathered around the two bookcases which'd fallen during the crime.

The cases had been propped upright, their tomes organized alphabetically once more as if nothing had happened.

Martha looked up from her book and pressed a finger to her pale lips. "Shush," she said, to the kids.

The group giggled again but moved further on down the line.

"That's in poor taste," Amy muttered.

"Kind of noisy isn't it?" Heather directed that at Martha, behind her desk.

Miss Rizzo huffed a sigh. "Kind of. These kids have been running amok in the library ever since it happened. The murder, you know. Helena just had to go and die in the middle of the library. Never good. Oh no, no. Never good to draw this kind of negative attention to a peaceful place."

Heather blinked. Amy narrowed her eyes at the teens at the end of the aisle. One of them picked up a book and chased a girl with it. She let out a girlish shriek and darted out of sight.

"Scandalous," Martha said.

"Miss Rizzo, I'm working with the Hillside Police Department to solve the murder of Helena Chadwick," Heather said, softly. "The sooner I solve it, the sooner the kids will lose interest in chasing ghosts around here."

Martha Rizzo pursed her lips into a wrinkled prune. "And you need my help?" She asked.

"Your cooperation would be appreciated," Heather replied, evenly.

An inner war rattled behind those wireframe glasses. Martha Rizzo glanced down at her book, then up at Heather again. "I was in the middle of a really good part," she said.

Amy folded her arms across her chest. Her lips writhed. Her bestie didn't think much of the response.

"All right, all right," Martha said and marked her place with a slip of paper. Light glinted from the square ring on her middle finger.

A diamond ring. Heather's heart skipped a beat. "That's a lovely ring," she said.

"This old thing?" Rizzo asked. "I've had it for years. Family heirloom. Anyway, what did you want to ask me?"

"You were here on the day of the murder, correct?" Heather asked.

The group of teens wandered past, back out the front door,

whispering to each other and joking around. Silence fell after their exit. The sanctity of the library resumed.

"Yes, I was here. I heard the crash when the bookcase fell over," Rizzo said and adjusted her glasses between two fingers. "If you ask me, Helena Chadwick asked for it."

"What? What do you mean?"

"She was in trouble," Martha said and leaned toward the front of her counter. She pressed both palms to the top of her book. "She came in here each morning looking paler than she did the last. I'm telling you, someone was after her."

"You saw someone hanging around?" Heather asked.

"Oh yes," she said. "A guy with a Mohawk. I asked Helena about him once, and she just kind of, well, she gave me this look which gave me the creeps. Like I'd crossed the line," Martha said and creaked back in her chair. "She was dangerous."

"Dangerous."

"That's right. She had a history, and I wasn't happy when she joined us at the library. Having a history like that brings trouble. I was right, wasn't I?" Rizzo said. "I'm always right about things like this."

"And so modest," Amy whispered, loud enough for just Heather to here.

"All I can say is I know trouble when I see it, and whatever Helena landed herself in was the kind of trouble that stuck. It followed her from wherever she came from. Dallas, I think."

Heather made a note of it. She'd have to check that out later. Ryan hadn't been able to find Helena's next of kin, yet. The woman's history wasn't shady. It was pitch black.

"Thanks for your time, Miss Rizzo," she said.

"Uh-huh. Just you be careful, now," Martha replied and flipped open her book.

Heather shuddered in spite of the 'care' in the sentence.

Chapter 10

Dave curled up in Eva Schneider's lap and snored, happily. He flicked one ear to dismiss an imaginary fly, then settled again. Eva's small hands stroked the back of his furry neck. "A ring?" She asked.

"That's right," Heather replied. "She wore a ring. A diamond ring. Now that I know the diamonds are relevant, they keep popping up everywhere I go."

"That's easy to say if you went to a jewelry store," Amy said. She rammed her thumb into the button on the side of the DVD player. A new one which Eva had bought along with a small, flat screen TV.

"Are you having trouble dear?" Eva asked.

"I'm going to give this thing trouble in a second," Amy replied and poked the button again.

Lilly clattered around in the kitchen. Heather had offered to help her make the hot chocolate, but Lilly liked doing it on her own. Cooking and baking were two things she'd for which she'd developed a passion.

"You think I'm being unreasonable about the diamond ring?" Heather asked.

"It's difficult to say," Amy replied, and gave a triumphant battle cry. The DVD tray slid out from the side of the machine. "Think about it. We don't know what shape Helena's engagement ring was. There might not be a connection between her ring and Martha Rizzo's."

"But there are so many diamonds," Heather said and massaged her forehead. "It's like I'm seeing signs."

"As long as you're not hearing voices," Amy replied.

"Only yours Ames, and that's enough to drive anyone crazy."

Amy stuck out her tongue and inserted the DVD into the tray. She pressed the button again, but the thing didn't close. "Oh for heaven's sake."

Heather rolled her tongue along the back of her teeth. She smacked her lips. "Eva, you're sure you didn't see Martha anywhere near the bookcases?"

"No dear, I'm not sure at all. I saw her go back past them and toward the Ancient History section, which is in the back, nowhere near the crime scene, per say. After that, I didn't look out for her, anymore," Eva said. "I'm sorry."

"Don't worry about it," Heather replied. "How could you have known it would matter at the time?"

But the diamonds, they did matter.

"The diamonds don't matter," Amy said as if she'd read Heather's mind.

"Don't make me fight you, woman." Heather rapped her knuckles on her forehead. Eva's sofa was even comfier than hers, but she couldn't settle into its floral-upholstered arms without thinking this through.

Lilly whistled a tune in the kitchen and Dave's ears flick-flacked. He let out a muted, sleepy bark. A 'ruff' of acknowledgment.

"Tell me about the diamonds," Eva said.

Amy kept her silence, for once.

"Mr. Krakowski, the jeweler, was robbed a few days before Helena's murder, and when we went to speak to him, he claimed that she'd robbed him," Heather said. "You didn't see him in the library. Right?"

"No. I would've recalled the top hat," Eva said – the woman with her thumb on the pulse of Hillside high, low, and middle society.

"And Helena had a diamond tennis bracelet on her arm. An

item that may have been stolen from his store," Heather said.

"Where does the ring fit in?" Eva asked, and stroked Dave again. Her blue hair bobbled each time she talked or moved.

"The ring, well, it seems someone removed Helena's ring from her finger," Heather said.

"Removed? Maybe she took it off herself," Amy said and poked the button over and over again.

"Maybe. Or maybe, the ring on Martha's finger is the one and same. She might've stolen it from Helena," Heather said.

"But what's that go to do with the robbery at the jewelry store?" Eva asked.

Heather opened her mouth to reply but stalled. She wriggled her nose. "I – I don't know. I'm stumped."

"That's because it's not relevant. I'm the first to tout your investigative prowess, Mrs. Shepherd," Amy said and mashed the button again. "But this time, I think you're reaching. I think you're frustrated by the lack of evidence."

"You're not wrong there," Heather said.

The DVD tray finally slid closed and loaded. "Ha! Success!" Amy said, and Dave woke up fully this time.

He let out a terrific bark.

"Shush," Eva said and tickled his ribs.

Dave quieted under her gentle touch.

"I'll figure it out," Heather said. "I just need more time. And more evidence. And more motive."

"With a side order of onions," Amy said.

"Ew, who wants onions?" Lilly traipsed into the room, carrying a tray of mugs, filled to the brim with hot chocolate. Tiny white pillows bobbed on the surface – mini-marshmallows to complete the drink.

"Not me," Heather replied. "Those look delicious."

Lilly handed a mug to each of the adults, then settled down beside Heather. Cupcake hopped up beside her and curled into a ball, purr mode activated.

"There, it's starting," Amy said and hurried to her seat.

The title screen of Stardust flashed onto Eva's TV. Heather focused on the movie, but her eyes glazed over.

Diamonds. Diamonds everywhere. Why couldn't anyone else see them?

Chapter 11

Lilly dawdled down the porch stairs, her backpack in one hand and a bottle of iced tea in the other. She yawned without blocking it.

"Didn't sleep well?" Heather asked, and unlocked the Chevrolet with a click of a button.

"No," Lilly said. "I think I'm too excited for Nicolas' party. I think about it all the time. I want him to be happy."

"He will be, hon."

"I wish he went to the same school as me," she said and yawned again.

Heather opened the driver's side door, and Lilly opened hers too. They slipped into their seats and grabbed their belts, then clicked them into place. Lilly fumbled with hers a little, then sat back.

"Do you think those kids are happy?" She asked. "The ones at the shelter."

Heather started the car but didn't pull out of the drive just yet. "That's difficult to say. I think they're happier than they were before they arrived at the shelter."

"I guess," Lilly said and shrugged.

Heather's mind scratched for an answer. Her daughter had grown so much in the short months she'd lived with them. Lilly had changed mentally, and she'd sprouted up a few inches, too.

Vague, watered down answers wouldn't satisfy her. Her father had been a murderer after all – Heather had been the one to discover that.

"All right," Heather said and checked her seat belt. "You tell me something, Lils. Were you happier after you started living with Bill and Colleen?"

"I was happier there than before I was there," Lilly said, darting around the mention of her biological father. "I'm the happiest now because I have you and

Dad, and Ryan and Cupcake, and Amy and Eva and... and everyone."

"Because you love everyone and everyone loves you," Heather said.

"Yeah, that's right. So, maybe there are people at the shelter who love the kids too."

"Well, think about what the word 'shelter' means," Heather replied, and made a cradle out of her arms. "It's to shelter someone. To care for them. The kids there are cared for. They're loved in their own way, and that's better than where they came from."

"You're right," Lilly said and grinned at her. "I just wish they could have as much love as I do."

Heather glanced in her mirrors, and checked her blind spots, then reversed out of the drive. "That's the thing you have to remember," she said. "Everyone has their journey in life. They have their own little adventure to lead. All you can do is stay on your path and if you encounter anyone else, you try to help them out a little. Make their journey a little easier."

They drove down the road in silence. Lilly's slurped some iced tea out of her bottle and smiled at nothing in particular, her mood lighter after their little chat.

Heather turned right and cruised down a side road, past a few stores on the way to Lilly's school.

She slowed for the red light and Lilly switched on the radio.

Heather bobbed her head in time to the music and scanned the road, the sidewalk and –

She withheld a gasp.

Jones Krakowski stood just ahead of them, past the light, his arms folded across his chest, top hat nowhere in sight. He glared directly at Martha Rizzo, the librarian.

Why were they together? Jones hadn't mentioned Martha and

vice versa. Could the diamond ring have come from Krakowski's jewelers after all?

"Uh, mom?" Lilly tapped her on the arm.

"What is it, honey?" Heather asked, without tearing her gaze from the unsuspecting pair.

Martha folded her arms and took a step back, tears in her eyes.

"The light's green," Lilly said, just as a car honked its horn behind them.

"Oh shoot, sorry." Heather drove off down the road and flicked her gaze up to the rearview mirror to catch a glimpse of the librarian and her jeweler friend. Or were they enemies?

Too many variables. Too many questions.

"I'd like to help bake the donuts for Nicolas' party on Sunday," Lilly said, from the passenger's seat.

Krakowski turned his back and marched off down the sidewalk. Neither of them had seen Heather.

"Is that okay, mom?"

Heather switched her gaze from the rearview back to the road. "Of course. We can make them on Saturday in Donut Delights. You can pick the flavor. What does your friend like?"

"He likes chocolate. I think he'd like those Hot Chocolate Glazed ones you made before Christmas," Lilly said. "Maybe we could make some Strawberry Creams, too."

"Classic," Heather said. "We can do that." She focused on her daughter's words and the road. She had to force what she'd seen out of her mind until later otherwise she'd lose concentration, and that'd be dangerous.

Heather put on her indicator, turned right, and then stopped in front of Lilly's school. "Have fun, darling," she said.

Lilly reached across and gave her a side hug. "See you later alligator," she said. She opened the car door, grabbed her back, and then hopped out into the sunny morning.

The storm clouds had dissipated overnight. No lightning, no rain, and Heather had developed a killer sinus headache to add insult to injury. She waved goodbye to her daughter.

"What were they doing?" Heather whispered. "Why were they together?" She punched the off button on the radio and cut out the croon of a pop singer.

Probably not Britney Spears, but someone similar.

"Why?" She sat a moment longer. The school bell rang, and the kids disappeared inside. The parking spaces around her cleared of the Volvos and Audis. Everyone was off to work, but here she sat.

Heather shook her head to clear it of the deluge of questions. She started the car and checked her rearview mirror.

They'd been up to something, all right, and Heather would have to figure out what it was. First, however, she had to get to work and make a few donuts for the hungry masses in Hillside.

Those Pecans wouldn't sprinkle
themselves.

Chapter 12

Heather tied on her Donut Delights apron and smiled at the glazed beauties beneath the glass in front of her. Her grandmother would've loved the place. It was only a pity she'd never gotten to see it or bake in the kitchen.

She'd only just managed to force Krakowski and the librarian from her mind. It might've been a coincidence, or it might be something deeper, but she didn't have time to ponder it.

Donut Delights wouldn't run itself.

The kitchen doors barged open, and Jung rushed out of them,

chased by a cloud of donut and vanilla scents. "Heather," he said and waved. "I'm glad you're here."

"Me too," she replied and punched buttons on the coffee machine. She brought out two cups and placed them under either spout. "Coffee?"

"Not for me, thanks," Jung said. "I've got good news, though."

"Lay it on me."

"I've been speaking with a few web developers. The kind who develop professional looking sites, and I think I can get one of them to do our site for a little less than his usual price," Jung said.

He mimed firing an arrow into a bull's eye.

"Jung, that's fantastic!" Heather clapped her hands. "Oh wow, that will definitely help us increase our online orders." They'd dropped a little in that department of late, and Heather had had difficulty figuring out why.

She brought her steel silver beaker out from its spot and placed it beneath the milk frothing machine.

"Yeah, I'll speak to him about it and ask for a quote," Jung replied. "The minute I get more information, I'll let you know."

"Thank you so much," Heather said. "I really appreciate this." And it was the last thing she'd expected. She hadn't asked Jung to go ahead and find out more about the website.

A mere suggestion from the other assistants had chased him off in that direction. Ken had also made a big deal of carrying his camera around lately, and she'd caught him capturing a few snaps of the building from different angles.

No doubt, he was in on the whole website thing too.

"I'd better get back," Jung said and waved. He straightened his apron and strode back toward the kitchen doors.

Heather bent and grabbed the milk from the bar fridge, then straightened and sloshed it into the beaker. The great bonus of owning a donut and coffee store was the lifetime supply of donuts and coffee.

Cappuccinos remained Heather's favorite beverage, despite her new love of Chai tea. Heather made to turn on the milk frothing machine and fill the interior of her store with its buzz.

The front door crashed open, and the bell above it tinkled. A couple of shrieks cut through the rumble of chatter and coffee sipping. Customer's who'd been spooked.

Heather narrowed her eyes at the source of the disturbance.

Kate Laverne strode between the wrought iron tables and chairs, her gaze liquid fire. "Shepherd," she said, the sibilant words tickled Heather's nerves.

"You again?" Heather asked.

Amy would've had a field day with this one, but Heather had given her the morning off, along with Emily and Maricela.

"I've come to warn you, Shepherd," Kate said.

"You're always here to warn me, Kate. I've gotten bored of it. You don't have anything interesting to say?" Heather's finger itched toward the milk frothing machine's black dial.

She'd have loved to tune Kate out, but she owed her customers a peaceful atmosphere, and the minute the buzz of the machine sounded, Kate would match it with a few choice screams of her own.

"Go ahead," Heather said, in her best Clint Eastwood impression. "Make my day." Amy would've been so proud.

"You're not going to let my store in on the action at this fair of yours, correct?"

"For once, Kate, you are correct," Heather said. "Congratulations."

She couldn't help her anger at this woman. She'd burst in where she wasn't wanted and demand things she couldn't have.

Heather should've kept a cool head about it, but goodness she couldn't be perfect all the darn time.

"Then I'll give you this once chance to go back on that. One chance," Kate said and raised her bright red fingernail. She waved it underneath Heather's nose. "One chance only."

"Or what?" Heather asked, and closed her fist on that black dial.

"Or I'll sabotage your little event. I'll ruin it. Embarrass you in front of the entire town and everyone who comes to visit," Kate said, and a muscle hopped in her jaw.

"Oh, I see. So you're threatening me," Heather replied. "You do realize threats don't make me want to work with you, right?"

"I don't care what they make you want to do. The choice is yours. Bring in my cupcakes, or you're done, Shepherd. Done like a – like a –"

"Turkey?" Heather asked. "Donut? Silverside beef roast? I don't mean to be critical here, but the options are endless."

"Whatever. Make your choice. Me or you're over."

Heather didn't consider it for a second. No amount of threats or bullying would stop her from following through with the fair. She sighed.

"Well?" Kate crossed her bony arms across her chest and tapped her heel on the golden painted boards.

"I only have one thing to say to you, Miss Laverne," Heather said.

But she didn't say a word. Instead, she turned on the milk frothing machine and frothed the milk in her beaker.

Kate went pink as a plum. She threw her arms up in the air, spun on the spot and stomped off toward the exit.

Heather let the machine buzz a little longer to block out the tinkle and slam of Laverne's exit. At last, she switched off the machine and lifted the beaker. "The perfect foam," she said, "for the perfect cup of coffee."

She created her cappuccino and added a decorative swirl just for fun. On days like these, the little things counted. They added up to happy moments which she'd examine at the end of her evening.

Kate might have a plan to sabotage the fair, or she might be bluffing. It was something

Heather couldn't control, right now.

Neither were the odd facts in this case – and that bothered her more than Miss Laverne's temper tantrums ever could.

Chapter 13

"Just the cat this time," Amy said and stared at Cupcake's furry, white tail in front of them. "Not Dave?"

"Lilly, Dave, and Eva went to the shelter to visit the kids," Heather said. "Just because Cupcake can't go, doesn't mean she doesn't deserve a walk."

Amy harrumphed and kept her opinion to herself. It was better that way. The last time she'd commented on the kitty's presence on their walks, she'd ended up with scratches.

"Hey, that reminds me," Amy said. "Whatever happened to

Ryan's cat? Didn't he have a cat from his past marriage?"

Heather nodded. "Yeah, he did." She didn't like to think of the past much. "He had the kitty before I'd opened my eyes to how awesome they could be. I'll admit I was pretty biased at the time. I still feel ashamed about it."

"Oh gosh, what did you do to the cat?" Amy asked.

"Nothing," Heather replied and whipped her bestie's arm with the end of the leash. "Ryan gave the cat to one of his aunts. She lives over in Temple. He calls in to check on the kitty every now and again. Apparently, the two of them get on like a house on fire."

"Oh, well that's good. At least they're happy."

Heather still got a case of the guilt over that cat. She'd never asked Ryan to give it away, but he'd likely assumed she wouldn't want the cat in her house because she'd made it pretty clear she was a 'dog person' at the time.

"So where are we headed after the park? Krakowski's?" Amy asked.

"It's a little late for that. I just want to hang out for now. Gather my thoughts about the case. I've got to piece together the bits and pieces we've got, so I know which lead to follow next."

They paced down the sidewalk, the sun at their backs, and the park within their sights. The trees reared tall in the distance. A car rushed by and a man with a black Mohawk strolled down the sidewalk toward them.

Amy's eyes went round. "Heather."

"I know."

"Heather," she repeated.

"Act natural."

Amy swung her arms back and forth, a little too wildly for a natural walking stance.

"That's acting natural?" Heather hissed.

The Mohawk bearer ignored them completely. He kept his gaze on the space of 'crete between his feet and trundled along, the tips of his black hair undisturbed by the rush of air his passage created.

Mohawk man drew closer. Then he was beside them, passing and gone.

Heather turned her head to one side and eyed him out of her peripheral vision. Mohawk man didn't quicken his pace – why would he? He had no idea that Heather Shepherd had just honed in on her next interview target.

She bent and swept Cupcake into her arms.

"You're not going to –" Amy cut off and finally quit swinging her arms around like Coco, the gorilla.

"That's exactly what we're going to." Heather pretended to examine something on the ground and Cupcake meowed impatiently in her arms.

Mohawk man rounded the corner.

"He's gone left," Heather said and rushed down the street after him. "Quick Ames. Quick and quiet."

Amy didn't huff and complain for once.

They dashed toward the corner, then slowed and peered around the slatted wooden fence which bisected it.

The mystery man's Mohawk disappeared around the next corner.

"Left again," Heather said. "He's heading into the suburbs."

They followed him. Cupcake dug her claws into Heather's forearm and clung to her, but she didn't bother prying the kitty free. Her tail had formed a bottlebrush. Cupcake wasn't used to high-speed foot chases.

Heather peered around the next corner and caught sight of their target again. He walked up the short driveway to a low-slung home. No fence or gate and the garden was ill-kempt.

Abandoned? No. There were curtains in the windows.

He entered and shut the door behind himself.

"Well, that's where he lives," Amy said. "Are we done now?"

"Not even close," Heather said. "Hold my cat." She handed Cupcake and her magenta leash over and ignored Amy's moan of fear. Heather dug around in her bag and brought out her cell and her Taser.

"Oh boy," Amy said. Cupcake hadn't started scratching yet, at least.

"Let's do this," Heather replied.

The fading light didn't do much to hide them from view, and the mystery man's front garden didn't hold a tree or a bush for cover. They'd just have to confront him head on if it came down to that.

Failing that, she'd call Ryan to come check the guy out.

They jogged across the road, down the sidewalk, and up the garden path. Heather halted in front of one of the windows, just off the side of the porch.

Mystery Mohawk stood in the center of the room, beneath the ceiling light. He held a golden pocket watch in one hand, and a magnifying glass in the other.

Heather took another step forward and peeked at the coffee table below his knees.

Diamond tennis bracelets, necklaces, watches. The loot from the jewelry store heist.

The thief turned toward the window.

"Get down," Heather hissed and ducked beneath the sill. Amy followed her lead. Cupcake had the good sense to keep silent and claws away.

They'd just found the jewelry thief. The light from the window above her head cut out and Heather tilted her head back.

He'd just drawn the curtains. That had to mean he'd be in there, admiring his stash for a little while longer.

"I knew the diamonds were relevant," she whispered. They'd found a connection between the diamonds and the victim. But why?

Heather unlocked her cell phone. It was high time she called in the professionals on this one. And she could think of no better professional than Detective Ryan

Shepherd with the Hillside Police Department.

Chapter 14

Amy had already taken Cupcake back to the house, to wait for Lilly, Dave and Eva's return, and the purple dusk settled across the remnants of the grass in front of Mohawk man's house.

Ryan strolled down the sidewalk. He'd parked his car down the road to avoid unnecessary attention.

Heather stepped out from the neighbor's yard and walked beside him. "Just you? No backup? This is a jewelry thief, Ryan. Surely he'll have some means of defending himself."

"I doubt he's got anything," Ryan said. "This guy didn't burst into the store during broad daylight. He pulled off a calculated late night stealth job. Blazing guns and anger don't fit the profile."

"Fit the profile?" Heather asked. "Maybe you're right. But should you really risk that?" She couldn't quash the bubbling nerves or the parade of butterflies in her stomach. They'd diversified into a marching band and a choir, now.

A whole town of butterflies to drive her into anxiety.

"Okay, Mrs. Smarty Pants. I've got backup on the way, already. They'll be here in five."

"But you're going to go in before that, aren't you?" Heather asked, and the choir performed another flappy winged chorus.

"I learned from the best," he said and winked at her.

She had to relax. After all, Ryan was a paid police officer. This was what he did for a living. If he thought for a second he couldn't handle the situation. He wouldn't go in there.

"Wait here, please," he said, in his commanding cop tone. "I'll call you when it's safe to come in."

She'd get to come in? Perhaps, Ryan thought it'd be best to

interview the guy now, while he was on the back foot.

Her husband strode down the garden path, past the withered grass and empty flower beds, and up the front stairs. He knocked twice on the front door. He didn't announce himself as she'd witnessed in countless cop shows and movies.

The Knock and Announce Rule only applied if the officer had an actual search warrant for the premises. Ryan didn't, as far as she knew.

A minute passed.

The door opened inward and Mohawk guy appeared in the

doorway. He let out a girlish scream and raised his palms above his head. "Don't shoot," he yelped. "I didn't do anything. Don't shoot, okay?"

Ryan lifted his hand off his holster. "Turn around please, sir. Keep your hands in the air." Ryan patted the guy down for weapons. "All right, now put your hands behind your back. Just like that." He cuffed the suspect and escorted him into the building.

"I didn't do anything. Okay, look, those aren't mine. I just found them here," the man said.

"You can come in, Heather," Ryan called.

Heather's insides reformed themselves. She hurried up the path on jellied legs. Nothing had happened, but it may well have. Luckily, Detective Shepherd always had control.

She entered the house and wrinkled her nose at the scent of burnt food and layers upon layer of dust like unpolished antique knockoffs in a back alley store.

"In here," Ryan said.

She took a right and entered the living room she'd spied on ten minutes before. The diamond items, the jewelry, lay piled on the stained wooden coffee table, and Mohawk man, pale even in the yellow light, swayed in the armchair.

"Police brutality. Why am I being detained?"

"You're being detained because you present a threat to myself and this woman," Ryan replied. "It's my obligation to ensure this situation doesn't escalate."

"So I'm not under arrest," the guy said and eyed the diamonds.

"Don't count your chickens, buddy."

"That some kind of small town saying?" Mohawk asked.

"No, that's just a regular saying," Heather replied. Ah, she'd found her voice, at last. "What's your name?"

"You don't have the right –"

"She works for the police department, son," Ryan said, though Mohawk couldn't have been more than ten years younger. "Answer the question."

The suspect writhed against authority. He stomped his big black boots. "Mordecai Dyson," he replied. Mordecai was much better than the name Mohawk.

"You knew Helena Chadwick," she stated.

Mordecai froze. He gulped, and his Adam's apple bobbed up and down. "What's this about?" He asked.

"Did you know Helena Chadwick?" Heather asked.

"Yes," he hissed.

"You know she passed," she replied.

"Yeah," he said.

"You know she was murdered."

"I don't want to jump to any conclusions," Mordecai said and glanced from left to right. Shifty-eyed. Oh boy – could they rely on anything he told them?

"Jump to conclusions?" Ryan asked, and unbuttoned his holster. "She was crushed by a bookcase, Mordecai, the conclusion has already come and gone. We're just looking for the why."

A bit blunt, but Heather could work with that.

"Why were you at the library on the morning of Helena's murder?" Heather asked.

Mordecai's temperament withered beneath her gaze. His bad boy punk rocker look failed beneath questioning. "I — look, I didn't hurt her, all right?"

"Answer the question," Ryan said, coolly.

"I came to find her, all right?" Mordecai replied. "She was my girlfriend before she – before she ran away. I wanted to find her. I loved her. I loved her with everything, but she kept running from me."

"Why did you follow?" Heather asked.

"I just told you," Mordecai replied. "I loved her." He moved to the edge of the armchair, his eyes as bright as the diamonds on the coffee table. "I would've done anything to keep her safe."

"Start from the beginning, Mordecai. Why would she run away from you, in the first place? And where did she run from?" Heather asked.

A siren whooped outside. The backup had arrived. The minute those cops busted through, murder investigation time would be over. They'd book Mordecai for the theft, instead and keep him in their interrogation room.

Heather needed to feel this guy out before they swept him off to a cell.

"Dallas," Mordecai said. "We lived in Dallas. I think she was scared. We got into some trouble up there, and she ran."

"Diamond trouble?" Heather asked, and gestured to the coffee table.

"Uh-huh. She told me she was sick of the life. She wanted to start new," he said, and a slow smile crept onto his face. "But I followed her. I knew she wouldn't be able to resist another gift."

"A gift?" Ryan asked.

"Yeah. The best gift. But she still ignored me. She told me to leave. I couldn't leave, man. I loved her. I still love her. I —"

Hoskins strolled into the living room, larger than life and the average man. "Well, well, welly, well-o. What have we here?"

Heather sighed and retreated to the living room window. She'd hardly gotten the chance to interview the kid, and all she'd felt was anger and fear, and an overwhelming sense of need.

Mordecai had definitely stolen the diamonds. And he'd definitely loved Helena Chadwick.

But had it been the obsessive kind of love? The deathly kind.

Chapter 15

Heather rearranged her fluffy robe and tied it tight around her waist. She dragged the laptop toward her on the top of her dressing table.

She stretched her fingers across the keyboard but didn't type anything just yet.

"Diamonds," she said.

The connection was there. She had to figure it out, somehow. Ryan was still down at the station, interrogating the suspect. He'd call her if he found out anything new.

"A gift," she said.

What had Mordecai Dyson meant by that? He'd given Helena a gift. One she couldn't resist.

Heather shuddered. That in itself sounded ominous, but the man had genuinely seemed to love her.

Helena had a checkered past, all right. Heather grabbed the dossier beside her laptop and flipped it open. She rifled through the information and brought out Helena's rap sheet.

"Petty theft, armed burglary, aggravated assault," Heather said, out loud.

Krakowski had been right about her, as had Martha Rizzo.

"A gift," Heather repeated. "Come on, woman, think."

She stared at Helena's mugshot and exhaled, slowly.

"Mordecai stole the diamonds from Krakowski's jewelry store. He gave Helena a gift. One she couldn't resist," Heather said and tapped her thumb on the picture. "The gift could've been the tennis bracelet. That would make sense."

Or was it the removed engagement ring? No, that had to have been worn for quite a while to create tan lines. Then had Helena and Mordecai been married?

Heather put the dossier aside. "Helena Dyson," she said, as she typed the woman's name into the google search bar.

The results came up with a few Facebook profiles and Twitter accounts, but nothing else of use.

"Shoot," she said. "Okay, so Mordecai gave her a gift. He hung out in the library and he – he –" Heather raised her palms to her eyes and rubbed them, furiously.

For the first time in a long time, the lack of evidence, the leads, all of it, had her stumped.

She might not be able to solve this one. Where was Amy when

she needed a sounding board? Sheesh.

Heather picked up her cell. She unlocked it and scrolled through to Amy's number, then dialed. She put the phone to her ear.

"It should be a crime to call past 9 pm, you know," Amy said.

Heather grinned in spite of the situation. "Then lock me up. Are you busy? I need to talk about the case."

"I was just making a cup of tea, actually."

"You? Tea?"

"I know, I know. Col's influence has rubbed off on me. A cup of green tea before bed and I sleep like a baby." Amy's kettle boiled in the background. "Okay, so fire away, investigator Shepherd."

"Mordecai Dyson gave Helena a gift. They might've been engaged or married, but she took off her ring."

"So maybe the tennis bracelet was the gift?" Amy asked.

"Maybe. That's what I was thinking. But that doesn't really help me much here. He could've showered her with gifts, but that doesn't tell me whether he killed her or not."

"Okay, so what do you need?" Amy's kettle clicked in the

background. She opened and closed a cupboard.

"I need some kind of solid connection to the crime," Heather said.

"Krakowski was convinced that Helena stole from him, remember? Maybe he did it. Oh, but he had an alibi."

"Exactly," Heather said. "Unless he worked with someone else. Could he have asked Martha Rizzo to interfere?"

"Maybe, but she didn't look all the strong," Amy replied. "Not strong enough to push over entire bookcases."

"Yeah, but the killer used something for leverage." If only they could find out exactly what that something had been. "It could've been any of them."

"What about Mrs. Krakowski?" Amy asked, and clinked a teaspoon on her end of the line. "I know she was laid up when we saw her, but that could've been an act."

"She was at her home at the time of the murder, remember?" Heather asked. But something clicked in her mind. What had Mrs. Krakowski said? That she barely saw her husband, at all.

Why was that?

"Ugh, Ames, this is so frustrating. I need to figure this out."

"Maybe you just need more information about each of the suspects. We don't know much about any of them," Amy replied.

That irritation still bubbled beneath the surface, seething to get out of Heather's mind.

"I don't know what to do."

Amy stifled a yawn. "What you should do is sleep on it. There aren't that many connections in this case. If you find more connections it'll get easier."

"Connections," Heather said. "I guess. I think I'll see Mrs. Krakowski tomorrow. Talk to her about her husband's movements. I know he's involved somehow. I feel it in my gut."

Her gut hadn't been wrong yet, but there was a first time for everything.

"Take it easy, Heather. You'll figure it out. You always do."

"Thanks, Ames," she said.

They hung up at the same time. After years of friendship, they were in tune with each other like that.

Amy's words teased Heather. She'd figure it out. She always did.

"But what if I don't, this time?" Heather shut her laptop, rose and went to check on her daughter, fast asleep in her bed.

Chapter 16

Heather strode up the large stone steps which led to the Krakowski's front doors, Amy at her side. A brisk wind gusted between those trees – so much for breaking the breeze – and tugged at Heather's hair.

Amy shivered and rubbed her arms. "It's getting cold again."

"I'm shocked you can feel it through all those layers," Heather replied and shuddered alongside her friend. She pressed the intercom button and held her breath.

The case had kept her up half the night. Thoughts of bookcases and battered librarians had chased away sleep, no matter how many glasses of warm milk she drank. That'd only resulted in way too many trips to the bathroom in the early hours of the morning.

"Who's there? Jones? Jones is that you?" Mrs. Krakowski's voice crackled through the speaker.

"No, this is Heather Shepherd. I spoke to you a few days ago regarding the murder of –"

The golden door handles pressed downward, and the wooden slabs swung inward. Mrs. Krakowski stood before them, shrouded in a white, fluffy robe, her platinum blond hair piled on top of her head.

"You're not sick," Heather said.

"No," Mrs. Krakowski said. "Have you seen my husband?"

"No, ma'am, we'd actually come here to –"

"He's leaving me," the woman sobbed, and mascara blackened tears tracked down her cheeks. "My darling Jones is leaving me. He's leaving me for good."

Amy rushed past Heather and slipped an arm around Mrs. Krakowski's shoulder. "It's okay," she said, softly. "Don't panic."

"I – I –" The woman bowed her head, and the tears came thick and fast. Her body shook on the spot.

"This way," Amy said, and led her back down the hall, toward the living room they'd met her in a few days earlier. "You sit down, and Heather and I will fix you some tea or whatever you like. We can talk about it."

Amy's soft coos faded down the hall. She walked Mrs. Krakowski into the living room and out of sight.

What on earth had just happened? Amy never touched people she barely knew.

It was a little-known secret, but Ames had been bullied terribly in middle school. She'd built up a wall to new people and carried it around for years. Her Amy brand sarcasm was a defense mechanism not many people could tolerate, but Heather loved her for it.

This was unheard of.

What was it about Mrs. Krakowski's situation that made Amy react like this?

"Kent," Heather whispered. "Of course."

Ames' had felt the sting of a failed relationship.

"Uh, Heather?" Amy asked from beneath the archway which led into the living room. "You just want to stand there or –?"

"Coming," she said.

Heather raced down the hallway, past a grouping of packed bags, which had to be Mr. Krakowski's. A glimmer caught her eye – diamonds? No, it was just a cane.

A cane with a metal base scratched beyond belief.

Heather's eyes widened. Her fingers danced to the front pocket of her jeans where she'd hidden her cell.

"I don't know what to do," Mrs. Krakowski wailed.

Heather stepped back from the cane. She couldn't jump to conclusions just yet. Heather hurried through to the living room and halted beside the armchair.

Mrs. Krakowski's tears had slowed. Amy sat across from her and grasped the woman's hand in her own. "What happened? Start from the beginning. Sometimes, talking helps."

Mrs. Krakowski nodded and steeled herself. She puffed out her chest. "Jones came home late last night and came through to the living room. He usually brings me some medicine or a cup of tea, but this time he came with nothing but his top hat."

"What did he say?" Amy asked.

Heather hovered on the edge of the conversation. Listening for a change.

"He told me that he was in love with another woman and that he was going to run away with her," Mrs. Krakowski said, and her chin wobbled. "I don't understand. I just don't understand. I gave him the money to start his jewelry store, and he seemed so happy."

Amy sighed and patted the back of her hand.

"But then he stopped paying attention to me and the only way to get him to notice me was to – to – Oh, I'm pathetic."

"To pretend you were ill," Amy said.

"Yes. I admit it," Mrs. Krakowski said. "I know it's ridiculous, but it's – you have no idea what it's like to be left alone all day long without any company. All my friends left Hillside years ago. And now this. Now he's going to leave me for someone else."

"Why hasn't he taken his bags?" Heather asked.

"He said he has to go to the jewelry store to meet her," she replied and burst into tears again. "Can you believe he told me that? It's like he never loved me. He doesn't even care."

Amy scooched closer to the grieving wife and murmured words of encouragement.

Heather couldn't keep up with the sorrow. Her mind flicked ahead to Krakowski.

Krakowski's cane. Martha Rizzo with him on the street.

She'd never have guessed in a million years. Pure dumb luck had brought her to the Krakowski residence today.

"Ames, will you stay here with Mrs. Krakowski and make sure she's all right?" Heather asked.

Amy gave her a thumbs up but didn't reply. She whispered to the old woman, her own eyes shining with tears which hadn't spilled yet.

Heather wormed her cell phone out of her pocket, turned on her heel and marched out of the living room. She multi-tasked down the hall – cell unlocked, Ryan's number dialed, phone to her ear.

"Detective Shepherd," he said.

Heather snatched up Krakowski's cane as she walked. "Meet me at Krakowski's store, love. We've got our killer."

Chapter 17

The front gate of Krakowski's jewelry store stood open, and Martha Rizzo grasped the rails of the second gated door, her face pressed to it.

"You're crazy." Jones Krakowski stood inside the store, lit by the opulent chandelier above his head. He held another walking cane in his right hand and held it out at arm's length. "Get away from the door."

Ryan and Heather stood to the left of the store, out of the man's line of sight.

"You gave me a ring, Jones," Martha said, the sunlight glancing off her bright red hair. "A ring. That means we're forever. You know I'd have done anything to be with you. How can you act surprised."

"I can't believe I didn't figure it out sooner. I – you stole my cane."

"I brought it back," Martha said.

"The cops will think I did it if they find that cane. I can't do this. I thought you were the one," Krakowski said.

"Yes, and Helena got in the way," Martha replied, evenly.

Ryan crept toward the first open gate. He grabbed the iron bars.

Krakowski's eyes widened, and he whipped his cane through the air. "I swear, officer, I didn't kill her."

Ryan slapped the gate shut and trapped Martha Rizzo in the compartment. The other librarian spun around to face them, and her wire-rimmed glasses flew off her face and hit the wall.

"Miss Rizzo," Heather said and strode into the picture. "Care to explain that confession we just heard?"

Martha's jaw worked. Her mouth opened and closed. "I – she –"

"We found the cane," Heather said.

Martha's gaze sharpened. "Yeah, I killed her," she said, after a second. "She was bad news. Bad news for the library and bad news for the jewelry store."

"My jewelry store has nothing to do with this," Jones announced. "I swear I didn't know until this morning. I finally figured it out when my cane reappeared in the hall with scratch marks all over it. How did you get into my house?"

"Oh please, your darling wife always leaves the front door unlocked," Martha snapped and backed up against the wall. She switched her gaze between Jones and back to Heather and Ryan.

"Why did you do it?" Heather asked.

"She stole from Jones. She took the diamonds and all the money he'd saved for our plans to elope. To run from the city and his sick, boring wife at last."

Oh gosh, this was a mess.

"I wasn't going to elope with her," Krakowski replied, and the silver-capped cane trembled. "I told you that. I told you I had to stay and look after the store."

"Exactly. Helena needed to pay. I knew she'd only steal from you again. I knew the day I saw her wearing that diamond tennis bracelet on her arm," Rizzo replied and pursed her lips. "She wasn't going to stop until she bankrupted you."

"What?" Krakowski asked, and actually looked around his store as if to check nothing else had gone missing in the interim. "How do you know that?"

"I saw her meeting with an unsavory type. A guy with a black Mohawk. He was her accomplice."

Martha wasn't far off on that, but she'd gotten a few things mixed up.

"Helena didn't steal the diamonds," Ryan replied. "We have the thief in custody."

Martha Rizzo blinked. "Impossible," she said. "Impossible."

"Martha, if you believed Helena stole the diamonds from the store, why didn't you report it to the police?" Heather asked. "Do you doubt they can handle –"

"Jones reported it to the police. He reported it ages ago, and you people did nothing to arrest her even though everyone knew it was her," Martha said and drew herself up straight. "So I did what I had to do to get my boyfriend's assets back."

Except Jones hadn't reported the theft. And he hadn't gotten any assets back because the diamonds were still under lockdown as evidence in the murder case.

"I – uh, I might not have had time to report the murder," Krakowski said. "What with the wife being sick and all. I didn't, you know, I didn't have the time."

"What?" Martha asked. "You didn't – It doesn't matter. I made sure that you'd get your money back so we can run away together. It was a public service."

"A public service," Ryan said and pinched the bridge of his nose. The first sign of irritation she'd ever seen him express while in uniform. "There's something in the water around here. There has to be."

"What's that supposed to mean?" Martha asked.

"It means you're under arrest for the murder of Helena Chadwick," Ryan Shepherd said. "You have the right to remain silent —"

"I swear I didn't know until this morning and I couldn't call. I couldn't call because she cornered me here." Krakowski hugged the cane to his chest this time.

"Traitor," Martha yelled. "I loved you. I did this for us!"

Heather's stomach twisted into a knot. Ugh, this was so messy.

Mrs. Krakowski had pretended to be ill for Jones' attention, who'd been robbed by Mordecai to impress Helena. Jones hadn't reported the murder because he'd been too busy looking after his 'sick' wife, and Martha had taken matters into her own hands as a result.

Heather massaged her temples and shut her eyes to block out the scene.

Ryan touched her arm. "Go back to the car, hon. Your car. It's over now. I'll handle this."

He didn't kiss her, but the light caress gave her the strength she needed to turn her back on the messy scene and stride back to her Chevrolet.

Another case solved. Once again, the cost felt too high. It always was, when it equaled murder.

Chapter 18

Nicolas sat on a chair at the head of the table in the dining area at the Hillside Children's Shelter. He moved a makeshift plastic crown to one side on his dark hair and grinned at the kids who lined either side of the long table.

Donuts of every shape and color sat on plates across the table. Colorful milkshakes alongside them.

Balloons drifted in the corners of the room, happy smiles stretched across their plastic faces.

Lilly sat on Nicolas' right-hand side, grinning from ear to ear.

"She's happy," Heather said. "They're all happy."

Even though it was a really obvious thing to say.

"You don't seem all that happy, dear," Eva Schneider said, and linked her arm through Heather's. "What's the matter?"

"It's just the case," Heather replied and lowered her voice.

The laughter and chatter didn't blot out her words or Eva's, but she didn't want her morose attitude to ruin Nicolas' birthday party.

"What about it, dear? I thought it was solved."

"It is. Martha Rizzo is behind bars, and she'll stay there, it just, the whole thing made me sad, that's all."

"But why?"

Heather struggled to find the words for what she'd witnessed that week. She chewed on her thoughts. "I found it sad that Mordecai Dyson would've done anything for Helena Chadwick's love. That he'd stolen diamonds for her to get her back." Heather took a breath. "And sad that poor Mrs. Krakowski feigned being sick to get the love and attention of her husband."

Eva sighed and slipped her arm through Heather's. Her blue hair bobbled on top of her head as she nodded along.

"And it was sad that Mr. Krakowski would've run off with another woman he loved. That very same woman, killed Helena to gain Krakowski's affections." Heather shook her head. "None of it makes sense to me. Love is supposed to be beautiful and kind. I thought I had this figured out by now, and I don't."

Eva stroked Heather's forearm. "Oh, liebchen," Eva said. "Love is beautiful. And love can also be terrible. Nothing in life is ever one way or the other."

"What do you mean?" Heather asked.

"The same love which drives Lilly to create this special day for a little boy, a boy who has no family, is the same love which drove Mordecai to steal those diamonds and trigger the events which ended in Helena's death." Eva's delivered the words in a monotone, but not without kindness. "Love is a great power. Love is good, but it can be corrupted."

"I thought it was pure."

"It is pure, but it's like anything else. The gun in the hands of one man is protection, but in the hands of another it can be wielded with murderous attempted," Eva said. "It's not the love that's the problem, dear, it's the people who wield it."

"I can't help thinking that all of this could've been prevented somehow. Helena ran from her past life. Maybe she wanted to make something better of herself," Heather said.

Eva paused and nodded once. Another wobble of her blue hair. "Perhaps you're right. But everyone in life has their own journey. At least Helena experienced love before the end."

The words mirrored those Heather had spoken to Lils earlier in the week.

Everyone did have their own journey in life, and there wasn't a way that could be controlled. Choices were made. People were different, and the illusion of control which investigating gave her was just that... an illusion.

"At least," Eva said, "you're bringing some good into the world, Heather. That's all that counts. As long as you live your life as best you can. The rest falls into place as it was meant to be."

"A series of choices," Heather said. "A trail of breadcrumbs that lead back in time."

"Precisely," Eva replied.

Heather squeezed the elderly woman's arm. "Thanks, Eva. You always know exactly what to say."

"Well, I have to bring something to the table, don't I?" Eva brushed off her burgundy, knee-length dress. "When the beauty fades, the humor and the brains are all that's left. And then, maybe not even that." She winked.

Heather chuckled and turned her attention back to the celebrating children.

Lilly's grin shone from the group. She leaned in and whispered something to Nicolas, and the two of them burst out laughing.

"There you are," Amy said and bustled into the room. "You'll never guess what I just found."

"What is it?" Heather asked.

Amy brandished a bright pink flyer, printed in bold black print. "Kate Laverne's at it again. She's hosting a cupcake fair of her own. Next Sunday."

"What?!" Heather snatched the flyer from her friend – love and choices forgotten. "Oh my gosh."

"This must've been what she threatened you about," Amy said. "Why I ought to –"

"No," Heather said. "No, we're not going to get angry about this Ames." She scanned the Comic

Sans print. Goodness, she could've chosen a better font. The whole thing looked rushed. "We're going to fight cupcakes with donuts and tea."

"How? There's no way we can host two fairs at the same time," Amy said.

"We'll just see about that," Heather replied. She folded the flyer in two, then tossed it into the wastepaper basket nearby.

Kate Laverne had picked her battle.

And a battle royal it would be.

Heather's weapon? Donuts. And Amy's dry wit. And another week of preparation, of course.

But for now, Heather would enjoy the day and the time she had with her friends, and the little girl in pink, a dot of chocolate glaze on the tip of her nose.

THE END

A letter from the Author

To each and every one of my Amazing readers: *I hope you enjoyed this story as much as I enjoyed writing it. Let me know what you think by leaving a review!*

I'll be releasing another installment in two weeks so to stay in the loop (and to get free books and other fancy stuff) Join my Book club.

Stay Curious,

Susan Gillard

44732252R00121

Made in the USA
San Bernardino, CA
22 January 2017